THE CAT ON THE MAT IS FLAT

BY

ANDY GRIFFITHS

ILLUSTRATED BY TERRY DENTON

SQUARE
FISH

FEIWEL AND FRIENDS

NEW YORK, NY

SQUARE
FISH

An Imprint of Macmillan

THE CAT ON THE MAT IS FLAT. Text copyright © 2006
by BACKYARD STORIES PTY LTD. Illustrations copyright © 2006
by Terry Denton. All rights reserved. Printed in the United States
of America by LSC Communications, Harrisonburg,
Virginia. For information, address Square Fish,
175 Fifth Avenue, New York, NY 10010.

Library of Congress Cataloging-in-Publication Data Available
ISBN 978-0-312-53584-1
LCCN 2008300735

Originally published in the United States by Feiwel and Friends
First Square Fish Edition: September 2009
Square Fish logo designed by Filomena Tuosto
mackids.com
20 19 18 17 16 15

LEXILE: 630L

Contents

THE CAT,
THE MAT,
THE RAT,
AND THE
BASEBALL BAT

The cat sat.
The cat sat on the mat.

The cat sat on the mat
and as it sat
it saw a rat.

The cat jumped up
and chased
the rat

around
and around
and around
the mat.

The rat did not like
being chased by the cat,
and after three laps
around the mat

the rat said,
"That's enough of that!"
And it went
and got ...

a baseball bat.

The rat
chased the cat.

The rat
chased the cat
with the
baseball bat.

Around
and around
and around
the mat

the rat
chased the cat
with the baseball bat
until …

KER

PLAT!

Never again
did that cat
chase the rat—
the cat
was much too flat
for that.

ED AND TED
AND
TED'S DOG
FRED

There was a man
whose name was Ed.

Ed lived in a shed
with his friend Ted.

Ted had a dog
whose name
was Fred.

Ed liked Ted
and Ted liked Ed

and Fred liked Ted
but he didn't like Ed.

One morning Fred
jumped on Ed's bed.

Ed said, "Fred,
get off my bed!"

But Fred
just growled
and bit Ed's head.

Ed saw red
and then
he said:

"I'm fed up
with Fred
always biting
my head!

I'm leaving this shed."

And he went
to his car
(which
was
red).

He
jumped in
and away he sped.

Ted said,
"Ed! Come back to the shed!"
But Ed just shook his head
and fled.

So Ted jumped in his car
(which was also red).

But it wouldn't start.
The battery was dead.

Ted stamped his feet
and his face went red.
"Bother! Bother! Bother!" he said.
"I'll have to take the sled instead."

Ted hitched up Fred
to the front of the sled
(which, by the way,
was also red)
and away
from the shed
sped Fred and Ted.

Ted and
Fred
sped
after Ed.

Ted saw
Ed's
red car
up ahead.
"Faster,
faster,
Fred!"
said Ted.

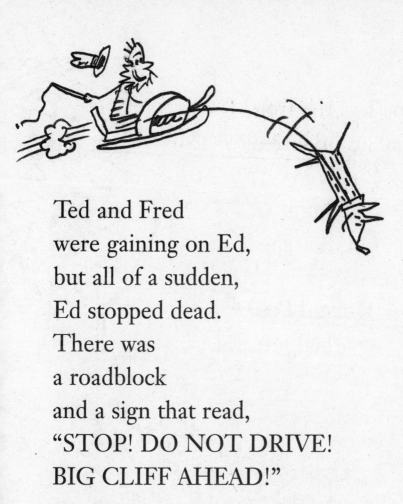

Ted and Fred
were gaining on Ed,
but all of a sudden,
Ed stopped dead.
There was
a roadblock
and a sign that read,
"STOP! DO NOT DRIVE!
BIG CLIFF AHEAD!"

Ted said, "Fred!
Stop the sled!"
But Fred
could not.
On they sped!

Ted and Fred
smashed into Ed.

Over
the
cliff
Ed
plumm-et-ed!
Closely
followed
by
Ted
and
Fred.

They
hit the water
and
sank like lead.
Poor Ed
and Ted
and Ted's dog
Fred!
They were
drowning
and
almost dead ...

when they were swallowed
by a whale
called
Ned.

"Bother!" said Ed.
"Bother!" said Ted.
"Woof! Woof! Woof!" said
Ted's dog Fred,
as they bobbed around
in the belly of Ned.

Ed and Ted and Ted's dog Fred
were certain
they were surely dead,
but the
whale called Ned—
who was overfed—

blew Ed
and Ted
and Ted's dog Fred
out of
the hole
in the top
of his head.

36

Up,
up,
up,
flew
Ed
and
Ted.

Up,
up,
up,
flew Ted's
dog
Fred

and
then ...

down,
down,
down,
they all did
head!

"Oh no,"
said Ted
with deathly
dread.
"We'll hit
the ground.
We'll end up
dead!"

"Fear not,"
said Ed,
to his friend Ted,
stretching a
handkerchief
over his head.
"Hang on to me, Ted!
Hang on to Ted, Fred!"
And
down
to
the
ground
they
para-chut-ed.

"Thank you,
        thank you, Ed!" said Ted.
"Thanks to you we are not dead!"
"Woof! Woof! Woof!"
said Ted's dog Fred
as he jumped up
and LICKED
Ed's head.

Ed
hugged
Fred!

Fred
hugged
Ed!

Ted
hugged
Fred!

Fred
hugged
Ted!

Ed
hugged
Ted!

Ted
hugged
Ed!

And
they
lived happily
ever after ...
in their shed.

PINKY PONKY, THE SHONKY, WONKY, BONKY DONKEY

This is the story of Pinky Ponky.
Pinky Ponky was a donkey.

Tail

Pinky Ponky's tail was shonky.

Leg

Pinky Ponky's leg was wonky.

Pinky Ponky's brain was bonky.

And that's the story
of Pinky Ponky,
the shonky,
wonky,
bonky
donkey.

FROG
ON A
LOG
IN A
BOG

There once was a frog
who lived in a bog.

The frog rode around
on a jet-rocket log.
There was no faster
frog in the bog.

But then one day
while riding its log
the frog looked up
and saw a dog.
The dog
was riding
a jet-rocket cog.

"My cog is faster
than your boggy old log,"
said the dog on a cog
to the frog on a log.

"My log is faster
than your rusty old cog,"
said the frog on a log
to the dog on a cog.

"We'll see about that!"
said the dog on a cog.
"I challenge you, frog,
to a race round the bog!"

"I agree!" said the frog.
"It's you and your cog
versus me and my log ...

56

and I'm going
to beat you,
Dog-on-a-cog."

But just then
along came
the boss
of the bog:
a big, fat, hairy
slob of a hog.

"STOP!" said the hog
to the dog and the frog.
"Racing is NOT
allowed in my bog!
Not on a log!
Not on a cog!
No log-racing frogs!
No cog-racing dogs!
Do you hear me,
Frog-on-a-log?
Do you hear me,
Dog-on-a-cog?"

But the dog and the frog
just laughed at the hog—

and took off at high speed
around the bog.

The frog on a log
got in front of the dog!

Then the dog on a cog
got in front of the frog!

The frog raced its log
and the dog raced its cog
around
and around
and around the bog

until ...

up ahead
they saw the hog
standing on top of a
wall made of logs!

"Stop!" cried the hog.
"Stop, dog!
Stop, frog!
Stop this race around my bog!"

"But we're going too fast!"
cried the frog on a log.
"We CANNOT stop!"
cried the dog on a cog.

Crash! Bang! Pow!

Kersplog!

Into the air flew the dog and the frog.
Into the air flew the log and the cog.
Into the air flew the hog and his logs.

And then
down came the dog
on top of the cog!

Down came the frog
on top of the dog!

And last of all
down came the hog—
right on top of
the frog's
rocket log!

"Hey, this is fun!"
said the log-riding hog
as he rode the frog's log
past the dog and the frog.

"I'm the fastest hog on a log in the bog!
Try to catch me, dog and frog!
Try to catch me on the cog!"

"Okay!" said the frog.
"It's you on the log
versus us on the cog,
and we're going
to beat you,
Hog-on-a-log."

And so the dog and the frog
on the jet-rocket cog
spent the rest of the day
racing the hog ...

around
and around
and around the bog.

HARRY BLACK, THE SACK, THE SNACK, AND A SNEAKY SNACK-STEALING YAK CALLED JACK

There was a man
           called Harry Black.
Harry Black had a sack.
In his sack he had a snack.
He carried the sack
with the snack on his back.

One day while walking
down a track,
Harry Black met Jack the Yak.
"Hello, Jack," said Harry Black.

"Hello, Harry Black," said Jack.
"Is that a snack I can
smell in your sack?"

"Why, yes, it is,"
       said Harry Black.
"I carry a snack
in the sack on my back."

"Can I have some, Harry Black?"
said Jack the Yak, who had no snack.

"No way, Jack," said Harry Black.
"Get your own snack, Jack the Yak!"

"You'll be sorry,"
said Jack the Yak.
"You'll be sorry, Harry Black!"

But Harry Black
just turned his back
and kept on walking
down the track
until he saw
a big haystack.

"I think I'll have a little nap
and rest my sore and aching back,"
said the very tired Harry Black,
as he climbed the haystack
with his sack.

But while Harry Black
enjoyed his nap,
Jack the Yak
snuck into the sack
and ate up all of Harry's snack.

Then Jack the sleepy,
snack-filled Yak
fell fast asleep
in Harry's sack.

"Alas! Alack!" cried Harry Black
when he woke up—
opened his sack—
and found Jack the Yak
in place of his snack.

"Alas! Alack! What a setback!
My snack has been stolen
by a snack-stealing yak!"
said the very angry Harry Black.
"I'm going to give that yak a whack!"

But Jack the Yak
jumped out of the sack
and yelled, "Get back,
I've got a tack!
And it's a SHARP one,
Harry Black!"

"Alas! Alack!" said Harry Black.
"I cannot give that yak a whack!
Or he'll attack me with that tack!"

And then Jack the Yak
with his sharp tack
jumped out of the sack
and fled on horseback.

So ...

if you're ever walking
down a track
carrying a snack in a sack
on your back
and you meet a snackless yak
called Jack,
don't hold back:
Open your sack
and share your snack—

for Jack the sneaky,
snack-stealing Yak
might just have
a very sharp tack
and you could end up
like poor Harry Black—
alone and hungry
on a haystack
with nothing but
a snackless sack.

DUCK IN A TRUCK IN THE MUCK

There was a duck.
His name was Chuck.
Chuck the Duck
drove an ice-cream truck.

But one wet day Chuck's
truck got stuck.

"What bad luck,"
said Chuck the Duck.
"My ice-cream truck
is stuck in muck."

But just then
along came
his friend Buck
in his brand-new
shiny
muck-sucking
truck!

"Hey, Buck," said Chuck,
"my truck is stuck. My truck is stuck
in all this muck."

"You're in luck, Chuck,"
said Buck the Duck.
"I can get your truck unstuck.

I can suck up all the muck
with the muck-sucker-upper
on my muck-sucking truck!"

"Thank you, thank you, Buck,"
said Chuck.
"What are friends for?"
said Buck to Chuck.

Buck's
muck-sucker-upper
began to suck.

It sucked
and sucked
and sucked
and sucked
until all the muck
had been
sucked up.

"Hooray!" cried Chuck
as he ran to his truck.

"Get back, Chuck!"
yelled Buck the Duck.
"I haven't yet shut my muck-sucker up."

But it was too late
    for Chuck the Duck—
he got sucked up into the truck.

And then the muck-sucker
sucked up Buck!

The muck-sucker-upper just
kept on sucking.

It sucked
and sucked
and sucked
and sucked ...

until Buck the Duck's
brand-new truck
got too full and
it

blew
up!

Out flew Chuck.

Out flew Buck.

Out flew all the sucked-up muck.

"Boo-hoo," cried Buck.
"My brand-new truck!
My brand-new shiny
truck blew up!"

"Don't cry, Buck,"
said the kind duck Chuck.
"We can share my
ice-cream truck!"

"Do you mean it, Chuck?"
said Buck.
"What are friends for?"
said Chuck to Buck.

So Buck hopped up
with Chuck the Duck
and they drove off together
in their ice-cream truck.

UNLUCKY LOU,
A KIND KANGAROO,
A HOLE IN A SHOE,
AND SOME
EXTRA-SUPER-FAST-
STICKING
SUPER-ROO-GLUE

There once was a girl
called
Unlucky Lou:
the unluckiest girl
that the world
ever knew.

One day while visiting
at the zoo,
Lou found a hole
in the sole
of her shoe.

"Boo-hoo!"
cried Lou,
"what
will
I do?
If only
I had
some
superglue!"

"Don't cry, Lou,"
said a kind kangaroo.
"You can borrow
some of my
super-roo-glue!
It's even more super
than superglue
AND it's extra-super-fast-sticking too!"

"Oh, thank you, thank you!"
said Lou to the roo.
"Thanks to you
and your super-roo-glue
now I can fix
the hole in my shoe."

But while super-roo-gluing
the hole in her shoe,
Lou slipped and spilled
almost all of the glue,
and then she tripped
and fell in it, too.

"Boo-hoo!" cried Lou,
"now what
will I
do?

I've fixed the hole
in the sole
of my shoe,
but now I'm stuck
in all this goo!"

But the kangaroo
knew just what to do.

It jumped over the fence
and kicked poor Lou,
as hard as only a roo can do.

Out of the glue
flew Unlucky Lou.
Up into the air
she flew and flew!

She flew right over
the walls of the zoo

and landed headfirst
where a prickle bush grew.

Poor old prickle-headed
superglued Lou:

the unluckiest girl
that the world ever knew!

BILL
AND PHIL
AND
THE
VERY
BIG HILL

There was a man.
His name was Bill.
Bill had a friend.
His name was Phil.

One day Bill and his friend Phil
climbed to the top of a very big hill.

"I dare you to roll
down the hill,"
said Bill.

"I will if you will, Bill,"
said Phil.
"I will if you will, Phil,"
said Bill.

So Bill and Phil
rolled down the hill.

Faster and faster
rolled Phil and Bill.

"Help!" said Bill.
"I'm feeling ill!"
"Me too," said Phil.
"It's a VERY big hill!"

But Bill and Phil
kept rolling until
they landed in a puddle of

smelly pig swill!

"Yuck!" said Bill.
"Yuck!" said Phil.

"Do you want to do it again?" said Bill.
"I will if you will, Bill," said Phil.
"I will if you will, Phil," said Bill.

So ...

once more they climbed
that very big hill
and rolled back down
into the swill.

And then they did it again ...

and again ...

and again ...

and for all I know
they're doing it still.

ANDY G,
TERRY D,
THE BRAVE TEA LADY,
AND
THE EVIL BEE

One day while out walking
by the sea,
I saw a sign saying,
"BEWARE OF THE BEE.
YOU'LL GET STUNG
UNLESS YOU FLEE!"

But before I could flee,
I saw the bee.
And, even worse,
that bee saw me.

I had to run.
I had to flee.
As fast as my feet
could carry me.

As I ran I saw Terry D
and he looked up and he saw me.
"Why do you run so fast?" said he.
"Where are you going, Andy G?"

"The bee!" I cried.
"Can't you see?
That evil bee is after me.
From that bee I must flee
or it will surely bee-sting me."

"I see, I see," said Terry D.
"I see the bee.
I see that I must also flee.
I'll come with you, Andy G."

And so Terry D ran after me.

We ran and ran quite speedily.
We passed a lady selling tea.
"Why are you running
so fast?" said she.
"Won't you stop and have some tea?"

"No time for tea," said Terry D.
"We're being chased by an evil bee.
From that bee we must flee
or stung by the bee
we'll surely be."

"I see," said the lady selling tea.
"I see the bee.
I see that I must also flee.
Jump aboard my trolley with me.
It's a super-fast trolley
that is powered by tea."

And so we fled.
We fled, all three.
As fast as we could—
pursued by that bee.

But just as we were almost free
the tea trolley crashed
into a mighty tree.
"Quick!" said Terry,
"climb up the tree.
As fast as you can,
because here
comes the bee."

Up we climbed.
One, two, three!
Terry D, the tea lady, and me.
We climbed and climbed
and climbed, we three.

We climbed right up
to the top
of that tree
until there was
nowhere left to flee.

I turned to face our enemy—
that evil, nasty, stinging bee—
and said to it most angrily,
"Why do you seek
to sting us three?
Just buzz off and let us be."

But the bee just buzzed
with evil glee
and made a beeline
straight for me!

161

But I didn't get stung
by that evil bee
thanks to the tea lady's bravery.
She quickly jumped
in front of me
and waved her teapot
threateningly.
"STOP!" she cried,
"you nasty bee!"

But STOP
that nasty bee
DID NOT ...

and so she
trapped it in her pot!

"Yippee! Yippee!" cried Terry D.
"No longer will that bee fly free."

"Now," sighed
the tea lady
cheerfully,
"how about
that cup of tea?"

So we all sat down
at the top of the tree
and shared a pot
of fresh bee tea.

Go Fish!

GOFISH

ANDY GRIFFITHS

What did you want to be when you grew up?
A rock and roll singer.

When did you realize you wanted to be a writer?
When I realized I couldn't sing.

What's your first childhood memory?
Being chased around the bath by brown blobs.

What's your most embarrassing childhood memory?
Being chased around the bath by brown blobs.

What's your favorite childhood memory?
NOT being chased around the bath by brown blobs.

As a young person, who did you look up to most?
Wile E. Coyote from the Road Runner cartoon. He never gave up.

What was your worst subject in school?
Math. If only two plus two equaled five, I would have been a genius.

What was your best subject in school?
English. What's so hard about spelling hipppapotamuss?

What was your first job?
Cleaning up my bedroom. I got fired after my first day.

How did you celebrate publishing your first book?
I got a tattoo: one of the fish from Dr Seuss's *One fish two fish red fish blue fish.*

Where do you write your books?
Wherever I am . . . usually in an exercise book.

Where do you find inspiration for your writing?
In dangerous and/or embarrassing situations.

Which of your characters is most like you?
Andy Griffiths from the Just! series. It's largely autobiographical.

When you finish a book, who reads it first?
My wife, Jill.

Are you a morning person or a night owl?
I love getting up at 6:00 AM and going for a long run.

What's your idea of the best meal ever?
Pancakes with strawberries and cream.

Which do you like better: cats or dogs?
Dogs, of course. Cats are dumb. (Except for the smart ones.)

What do you value most in your friends?
That they laugh at my jokes. Even if they're not funny.

 SQUARE FISH

Where do you go for peace and quiet?
I close my eyes and concentrate on my breathing.

What makes you laugh out loud?
Great comedy.

What's your favorite song?
Happy Birthday to you/You live in the zoo/You look like a monkey/And you smell like one, too.

Who is your favorite fictional character?
Pinky Ponky, the shonky, wonky, bonky donkey.

What are you most afraid of?
Being chased around the bath by brown blobs.

What time of year do you like best?
Winter: It's much cozier to stay inside and write than in summer.

What's your favorite TV show?
Hannah Montana!

If you were stranded on a desert island, who would you want for company?
My wife.

If you could travel in time, where would you go?
Back to prehistoric times to see dinosaurs fighting. That would be cool.

What's the best advice you have ever received about writing?
Write as fast as you can without stopping or thinking about what you're writing. You can edit it later.

What do you want readers to remember about your books?
That they had a great time!

What would you do if you ever stopped writing?
Start again.

What is your worst habit?
Laughing at my own jokes.

What do you consider to be your greatest accomplishment?
Getting other people to laugh at my jokes.

Where in the world do you feel most at home?
Wherever I happen to be. But especially at home. Duh!

What do you wish you could do better?
Fix things when they're broken.

What would your readers be most surprised to learn about you?
That I'm three billion years old. It's not true, but I think my readers would be quite surprised to learn about it if it was.

Hip hip hooray! It's raining cows today!
Andy and Terry are back with another laugh attack.

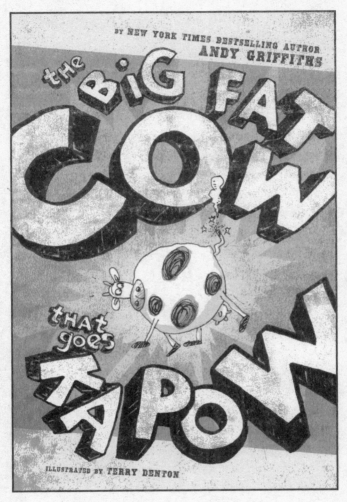

Keep reading for an excerpt from

The Big Fat Cow That Goes Kapow

available in hardcover from FEIWEL AND FRIENDS.

BIG FAT COWS

It's raining
big fat cows
today.

How many cows?
It's hard to say.

A big cow here.

A fat cow there.

Big fat cows are

EVERY

WHERE!

Cows underwater.

Cows in space.

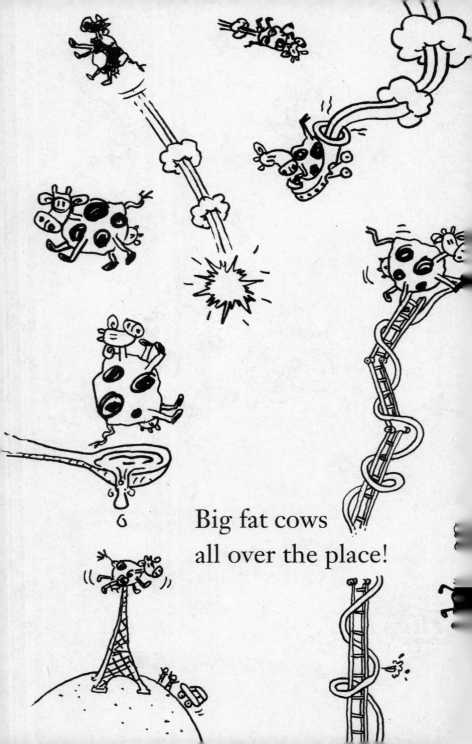

Big fat cows
all over the place!

Oh, no—watch out!

Don't look now!

This one is an

EXPLODING cow. . . .

Get ready for more
LAUGH ATTACKS

Written by Andy Griffiths
Illustrated by Terry Denton

978-1-250-03406-9

978-0-312-65301-9

978-1-250-01017-9

978-1-250-02690-3

978-1-250-